To Augustine & Christian

Victor Davis

2009

BABY WOLF

A WARRIOR'S TALE

BABY WOLF

A WARRIOR'S TALE

WRITTEN AND ILLUSTRATED
BY VICTOR DAVIS

NORTHBOOKS

Eagle River, Alaska

Illustrations by Victor Davis.

Published by:

ᗞORᏟᕼBOOKS

17050 N. Eagle River Loop Road, # 3
Eagle River, Alaska 99577
www.northbooks.com

Printed in the United States of America

ISBN 978-0-9815193-1-9

Library of Congress Control Number: 2008928171

DEDICATION

To my wife and family,
I love you all,
Thank you.

For my mother, one more adventure.

POEMS

INTRODUCTION

Hello, please allow me to introduce myself. I am the son of Arlene and John Hanson. My biological father, Victor, left this world nearly thirty years ago, and my mother just recently passed in November 2006 at only fifty-four years of age.

I am a unique case, as it were. For all intents and purposes, I am the last of my line of family. Yes, I do have extended family whom I love with all my heart, but as far as bloodlines go, mine ends with me.

My grandparents, Paul and Lorena Davis, both had children prior to their marriage. Their union gave us my father, Victor, who before the end of his young life married my mother and fathered me.

Life was not easy growing up without a father, but a good man assumed the role early enough to have an effect on my life and that was my step father, John.

I began writing these tales as a form of release. It also helped me with the grieving process as a way of remembering and honoring those who have passed, but also, those who are still with us as well.

What sparked the notion of a warrior's tale? Excellent question! For that you must go back with me to a time when I was only seven years old and still holding my mother's hand at a potlatch.

I remember seeing beautiful drums and paddles—and oh how the performers sang and danced! As I looked across the dancers' line, a question nagged at me. My grandfather and uncles are a proud people and they told me often, "Junior, always remember we are a strong people. We are known for our fighting ability and our fierceness in battle. Our warriors rarely lost a fight!"

As the dancers crossed my path, I realized my question, "Momma, where are the warriors?" My mother quickly pointed to the dancer at the front of the line and told me that was a warrior. I looked upon the dancer with a child's disbelief and said, "No, Momma, that's a dancer. Where are the warriors?"

Suffice it to say, I was scolded and that conversation never took place between us again. Yet something always bothered me from that moment on.

As I read history about our people, limited as it was at the time, even the books had little of what I was hoping to find. I still only found the occasional photo of a chief or a dancer holding a paddle, not the warrior I had imagined.

Life has a way of making you complacent, though, which I fear a lot of young people suffer from today, and I am certainly at the head of that line. For years I no longer questioned my past and simply walked blindly into my future, the way we all do in one way or another, ignoring the empty feeling in my heart. You know the feeling, something is missing, something is not right.

At one point in my life, I considered myself a fairly decent carpenter and made an excellent living doing so. My mother and I had a conversation which I will always remember because it was the last real talk we had before the stroke took away her speech. My mother said, "I love you and I'm proud of your accomplishments, but you are more than you are."

Shortly thereafter, our mother left us. This was the moment I finally woke up. Tragedy made me bold, and I realized I needed to change my path in life.

I did as much research as I could, and eventually found a book which spoke of the Russians' first contact with the Southeast people, and as I read, that's when I found what I always knew existed. In their text was an intricate drawing of a Tlingit warrior! He wore armor made of cedar, thick leather protecting his body, a short sword, and a beautiful cedar helmet. The warrior I had envisioned as a child. It was written that as the Russians made their way down the coastline, they were caught completely off guard by the sheer ferocity at which these natives attacked them and suffered severe casualties!

When I found this information, inspiration is the best word to describe my feelings, and I immediately thought of everyone I'd lost in life and realized I had work to do. I dove into this with all my ability and I hope to honor my family and my people.

These stories are for all the people who ask questions about their culture, yet get incomplete answers.

These stories are for the young people out there, who in one way or another, have been in a battle their entire lives, but do not know why.

These stories are for those of us who look upon the chiefs and dancers and know in our hearts that a member of our people is still not being represented to this very day.

These stories are for you, my family, from one of your last sons.

My parents named me Victor Davis.

My grandparents named me Gooch Yadi.

You may call me Baby Wolf, and I have a story to tell.

To sing, dance, drum.

To speak your heart, mind, soul,

and represent your people with honor is easy

when the number standing beside you is many.

But to do so when the your numbers are not,

therein lies true courage.

Baby Wolf

DEATH DANCES WELL

My wife,
Dancing Butterfly,
lays sick in her bed
I'm not sure she's heard
A word I've said.
I miss her smile
I miss her touch,
the shaman has said,
"We can no longer do much."
I'm a simple man
a brave, you see,
one day a warrior
I hope to be.
She's leaving me now,
I can only shed tears
and I know
I shall miss her
for all my years.
I cannot accept this!
This must be a mistake!
There must be some deal
I could make!
No sleep for days
I finally succumb.
Darkness envelops me
my mind and body go numb.

"Baby Wolf."
A terrible voice beckons,
I see a sight
I can no longer reckon
I know this place!
I know this place well.
It's where the demon with no face
chooses to dwell.
He has no form,
he's different to all
but face him in battle,
and you shall fall.

It hisses at me—

"I know your story
I know your plight
come with me
and do not fight.
Take her place
and come with me,
I accept your bargain
I will set her free.
She will live long
many more years than before
she will have happiness
all that and much more.
You, though, my son,
so young, so bold
your story is over
before ever been told!
It is done, you are mine.
Destined to stay here,
where the sun cannot shine."

"Foul creature!" I shouted
showing no fear,
"Thank you for sparing
whom I hold most dear.
I shall not fight you
as one might expect,
my story is over
in this you're correct.
Foul creature, you've won
the deal we've made
cannot be undone.
However, foul creature,
before the abyss
take one moment
and remember this,
I am Baby Wolf.
I have no equal, you see,
I go willingly now,
but you could never best me!"

A wicked smile appeared
where a smile might be
the demon let out a sound
that might have been glee.

Without hesitation,
it leapt and clawed
it showed me quickly,
my bravado was flawed.
We fought forever.
The demon gave ground never.
I could not win this impossible endeavor.

The demon snarled
and finally snapped,
"Fight! Fight! Baby Wolf!
You cannot win!
It's been you who I'm after,
not your kin!"

How long we fought
I cannot tell,
but what I do know now
death dances well.

The demon strikes
and is heavy handed,
the final strike
is what just landed.
I'm finished,
it's over—
the end of my life—
funny this is
I think only of my wife.

The demon smirked
at this waste of its time,
but in my suffering
it found something sublime.
It hesitated—
then time stood in its place,
I then heard a voice
I could never misplace.

"Baby Wolf, Baby Wolf
you must not give in,
you must not give up,
for that is a sin.
You're more than you know.
You're more than you are.
You're better than this creature by far!
You are not weak!
You are not done!
You will win this fight
for you are my son!
Now rise, Baby Wolf,
rise and fight!
Face this creature
and have not a fright!
Face him, my son,
and have not a regret
remember, my son
you are not done yet!"

The demon struck
with all it was worth—
strangely, I felt none of its girth.
Where the demon claws struck,
armor appeared.
The demon jumped back
roared and sneered.

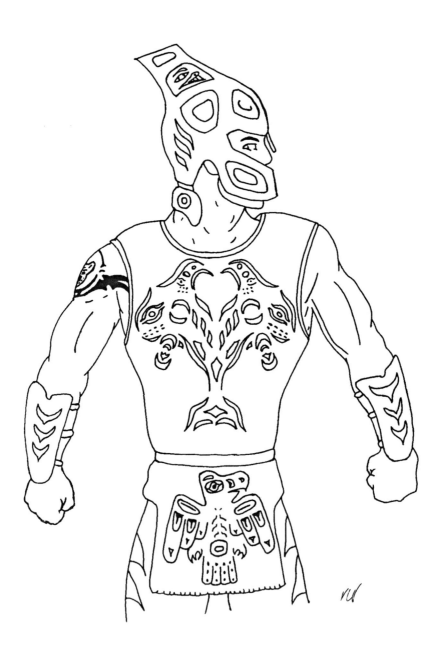

The armor was like none that I'd known,
none that was made, none that was shown.

I knew now
what I was meant to do
and stated,
"Come demon,
you and I are not through!"

It attacked again,
as fast as it could,
it went for the kill as I knew it would—

A shield appeared
in what was empty space,
the demon struck it hard
with its would-be face.
It staggered back—
confused! Enraged!
Not prepared
for what was about to be staged.

I charged the demon
to its surprise,
it never thought
of its own demise.

I lashed out with an empty fist,
but something arrived
almost from a mist—

A beautiful blade
like no other
Armor
Shield
Blade
A last gift from my mother.

I swung the fine blade
it struck and struck true.
The wicked demon
had been run through.

The demon lie there
wheezing and rasping,
At its final breath
it was grasping.

I had won
an impossible feat,
love taught this demon
about defeat.

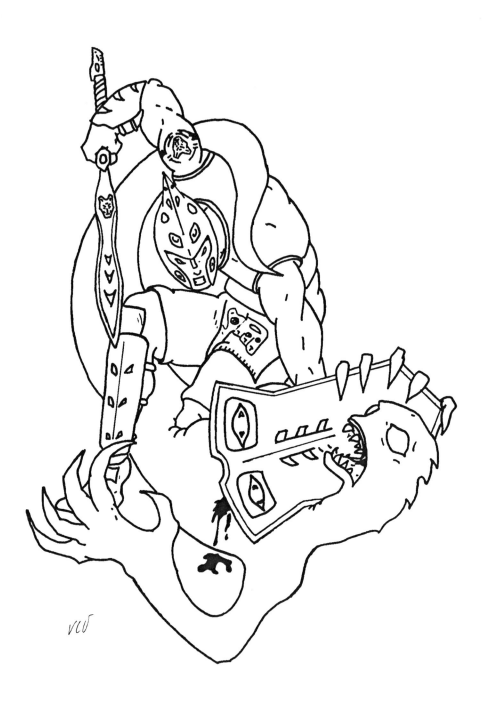

14

I stood over it
with its throat to my shield
and stated quite clearly,
"Foul creature... Yield!"

"Baby Wolf! Baby Wolf!"
Came a cry from a far away place,
came from a voice I could never misplace
"Wake up! Wake up! I miss your face!"

I felt my wife's hand touch my face.

Shamans were shocked—
No
Amazed!
They all walked around
practically dazed.

My wife had returned
from a place near dead—
they were not quite ready
for her to jump from her bed!

She hugged and kissed me
more than I could wish for or believe,
she made me a promise she'd never again leave.

Our families rejoiced
whooped and cheered
a time for celebration
finally appeared.

The end of the day
my Butterfly walked to my side,
and asked as wives do
"What is it you hide?"
As she looked upon me
with her worried brow
I will love her forever as I do now
I said,
"Worry not for me, my love, my spirit, do not fret,
always remember that we're not done yet!"

Never a Time or a Place

Years have passed
since that dark place,
time always passes
like its running a race.

I'm older now,
a warrior you see,
that which I've always been
destined to be.

Baby Wolf is my name
my innocence far gone
our chief informed us
this morning
the war is on.

I ready my warriors
so brave and true,
no matter the orders
they see them through.

In battle
I've seen men rise,
I've seen men fall,
truth be told
I live for it all.

My abilities proceed me,
if there is such a thing,
all know who I am
and that which I bring.

I do not sing,
I do not dance,
too much happiness
the elders cannot chance.
I am the weapon
they choose to wield
when it comes to war
and the battlefield.

I have lost a battle—
but only one—
against a demon
it now calls me
Son.
With my mother's aid
I handed it defeat,
but an accord
we did happen to meet.

My mother loves me
and showed a
life without wrath,
the demon shows nothing
except the war path.

I've faced countless enemies,
the ending always the same—
they all fall before me,
I care not their names.

My armor, shield and blade
are known throughout,
their effectiveness in battle
never in doubt.
I know I made them
with my hands,
but they do not come
from these lands.

A gift from my mother
a desperate attempt to save me
I wonder if she regrets that
and how gravely.

As we load the canoes
and prepare,
a voice—
my weakness—
catches me unaware.

"Baby Wolf!"
my Butterfly said with a cry,
"Don't you dare leave
without saying good-bye!"

I hold my wife close,
she holds back her tears,
I do my best to calm her fears.

"Baby Wolf, please do not leave this day.
Do what you must, but please, husband, stay!"

"I do what I must
to protect all I love
to the people before me,
to the spirits above.
This is my path,
this is my way,
to battle is where I am due today."

My Butterfly is barely half my size,
but she is a warrior's wife,
so anger is of little surprise.

"The Elders are wrong!
This you know.
They wield you as a weapon,
for it,
you have nothing to show.
They love you not,
as I do,
look in your heart,
you know this to be true.
This is not your way,
this is not your life,
leave that path alone,
stay here with your wife.

Yes, battles are fought,
battles are won,
but when Baby Wolf,
will yours be done?
If not for me
and if for no other,
then please, Baby Wolf,
please,
remember your mother."

Her words cut deep
as any blade.
Her point was clear
and very well made.
What have I done?
What have I become?
A hero to most
but a destroyer to some.
My wife was right,
this is not the way.
The demon no longer
held its sway.

"My wife, you are right,
after the set
of today's sun
my battles are over.
Finished.
After today, I am done."

We spoke for awhile
and at last embraced.
Now it was my retirement
I desperately chased.

We paddled away,
I do not look back.
I must focus on battle,
and proper forms of attack.

I am in the lead canoe
standing front of the bow,
we are near the rival village—
not long now.

I have heard of their leader,
Eagle Claw, their chief.
His feats match mine,
though I still hold disbelief.

As we approach the shore
I see all I need
and more.
Eighty warriors are on the banks.
I only have fifty—
to my elders I give no thanks.

I see Eagle Claw at the head of the line,
he has fashioned an armor
similar to mine.

I see him smile?
No.
A baring of teeth,
a hatred for me
apparently does seethe.

As the bow touches beach

I'm the first to jump ship,
but as I touch ground
my mind does slip.

I am back at home
with a loving wife,
no more fighting,
a normal life.
A potlatch is today,
Eagle Claw, my good friend,
is on the way.
Our clans are no longer rivals
but instead,
we are friends,
we are family,
we only break bread.

I snap back to the moment
and find I resent
what the vision has shown me
and what was truly meant.

Today I face a fellow death dealer and may die,
for rumor has it
he is stronger than I.

Now that all the canoes are landing,
it's time to see
who is the last man standing.

After my brief moment of clarity,
I now do battle
with my inner charity.

This is not my path—
not the path of my mother.
Who can justify
the attack on a brother?

My blade arm is heavy,
my confidence shattered,
I wonder if this battle
really mattered.

I was once a death dealer.
The one dance I knew—
there was not a war
I had not charged through.

I now realize all my mistakes
and now must correct them—
no matter what it takes.

Our people are beautiful, brave and free,
it is their given right just to be.
We have many temptations to resist,
why make each other fight
to simply exist?

I see our families
growing and caring,
protecting our culture,
our wealth we keep sharing.

Today, today is my last fight.
I will lay down my weapons
after this night.

Eagle Claw charges me as I advance,
he may be a great warrior
but he has not a chance.....

We are a beautiful people, if we try.
We all live for a while,
but inevitably die.
What you do with your years
is solely your making—
live for your people
life is yours for the taking.

Why o' why can't our leaders
just let be?
Set their differences aside,
let their spirits soar free.
O' why can't the elders and chiefs finally see,
there is never a time or a place
for one such as me.

MAKE ME A RATTLE

He is Eagle Claw—
maybe the best warrior I've fought—
perhaps he's my punishment
for all that I've wrought.

He is relentless and fearless—
dare I say maybe peerless.

One strike from his blade
I slide back six feet!

Rumors say he has not known defeat.

From the start
my situation was dire,
the strength of this warrior I can't help
but admire.

He strikes me again, his men let out a cheer.
This time Baby Wolf actually knows fear.

This giant
Animal
Man
Warrior
Will not stop.
My arms grow tired.
My shield does drop.

Eagle Claw raises his blade
sensing an ending nearby.

I then see a figure from the corner of my eye.
It's a young maiden hidden from sight.
A slave girl full of worry and fright,
she wears a crest, one I recall
but from where or when, I know not at all.
She's not of our clan, and not of theirs.
But the crest I know, the one she bears.
The young girl cries

"Baby Wolf you must live!
Raise your shield!
Raise your blade!
Live to keep your promises made!
You must finish this fight!
Finish this and make all your wrongs right!"

Eagle Claw swings
and swings wild,
but my only thought
is the life of the child.

I want to tell him
he is my brother,
to end this foolishness,
not destroy one another.
I see in his eyes
he's determined our fate;
His mind is set
it is already too late.

My strength renewed
my faith intact
it is now my turn
to finally act.

I dodge Eagle Claw's strike
and its fatal intention;
the tide of this battle
now flows in a new direction.

My foe flies past me,
but his blade catches my side.
I spin and face him—
live or die?
I decide.

I strike Eagle Claw—
a quick strike just to maim—
he will survive this
but forever be lame.

His men hear his cry,
look for their chief.
I will always remember
the sound of their grief.
To them I know
this is a very small token,
but I wish they knew
my heart is now broken.

I charge their clan,
warriors chant my name
our foes retreat,
retreat with shame.

This was a falsehood—
indeed a bluff—
I had charged our rivals
hoping it would be enough.

As my warriors
gave chase
over the hill,

I stopped,
stood silent.
Stood silent and still.
I look down and see
sand and mud
grass and blood.

My father always said
"Baby Wolf, you are too bold."
I remember his warnings
as my blood leaves me,
I'm cold.
Eagle Claw will get all he desired,
this deep wound in my side proves
my luck and life have expired.

40

I take slow breaths.
So this is all there will be,
I'm full of regret
as my life does leave me.
I kneel down
I'll leave with no loved ones by my side,
will never have children,
my fate sealed because of pride.
I lie there and wait
this is my end,
then who is at my side
but my newfound friend.

She lifts me up
I lie in her lap
with her hand on my face, says
"Do not take that long nap."

I attempt to stand, yes,
I do need her help
she's very strong, for a little whelp.

"Quick! Baby Wolf! Quick!"
She pushes me with a heave
the opposite direction of my clan
we do leave.
"Where are we going?
What do you intend?"

"Baby Wolf, you are dying
it's your wound
I must mend!"
We ran through the woods
into a clearing,
my world was getting dark
I felt death leering.

"Here, quickly lay down!"
I dropped to be true.
She's just a young whelp,
what help could she do?

"You're just a girl, what could you possibly know?"

"Well, for one thing," she replied
"I know how to sew!"

As the young one produced a needle and thread,
my world goes dark, yet I know not dread.

Darkness has me.

I awake suddenly and stir
"Are you delirious? Lay back and rest, sir!
You have been asleep for two days,
your mending goes well,
you should fully heal
as far as I can tell."

"What of my people?
What of my men?"

"Rest, Baby Wolf, rest.
Heal and you'll go home then."
Yes, she is right, I quickly drift away,
when I wake, it is a new day.

I awake to her tending a fire and singing a song.
I barely noticed, I was humming along.
The words of her song, sweet and sincere.

I slowly get to my feet, my vision becomes clear.
"Your strength has returned,
a very good sign.
We must return you to your village
and then me to mine."
I smile and nod in agreement.

I'm sure my wife does not enjoy bereavement.
I slowly walk, my legs unsteady
I begin to wonder if I am ready.

"Here let me help you,
we have a long trip.
Lean on me I won't let you slip."

This young girl,
she was Eagle Claw's slave?
How could that be?
She's as strong as a brave.

After a while we do talk,
it takes my mind off the painful walk.
She looks up at me
and says with slight mock,

"Your armor so damaged.
Scars proving you fought to survive.
Baby Wolf, please tell me
how is it you are still alive?"

44

I look at her and tell her my life,
about all my battles and about my wife

"As for the old injuries and scars you see,
I'm just the best warrior that I can be.
But truth be known,
I've survived mainly by bravery and luck."

She replied,
"Perhaps then, great warrior, you should learn how to
duck?"

For the first time in years,
I can't contain my laughter;
I'm sure this was the response my young friend was after.

We walk across the banks
across the tree line.
O' how today's bright sun does shine

We slowly walk through an empty village,
my warriors were thorough on their pillage.
We happen upon
a questionable boat,
but as my father says,
"Hope floats."

We board the canoe
and row away.
I smile, shake my head,
and to myself say,
"Baby Wolf's last battle
but a girl saved the day!"

After awhile, my home we did near,
my village was quiet,
not one person did I hear.

We beach the canoe
and walk toward my dwelling,
I glanced at the once talkative child and said,
"You look worried, young one,
what is it you're not telling?"

"Baby Wolf, do promise that war was your last,
your days as a destroyer
well in your past?"

"Yes, young one, with all my heart.
In another battle
I will never take part."

Her frown disappeared
She then grinned slyly,
"When you introduce me to your people
you'd best speak of me highly!"

"I will, I will, young one,
you have my word.
Your happiness and freedom
are well assured.
Young one, you have done for me
more than I can repay
I thank you now,
but feel there is more I should say.
Because of your kindness
I will see another day.
How can I repay the one
who saved me from my last battle?"

A moment of silence
she then said,

"Make me a rattle."

I attempt to give a puzzled look
for her request,
but as I turned toward her
I lost sight of my young guest.
I looked up and down the shoreline
and try as I might,
my young friend had vanished,
vanished from sight.
I took a deep breath and prepared to shout
but I thought for a moment,
which established a doubt.
I looked at our path
saw only one set of tracks—
I concluded then
this is not how a sane man acts.
What had happened these past few days?
What had occurred?
The more I thought about it
the more I felt deterred.

As I stood and contemplated my sanity
a sudden burst of movement startled me
and I nearly let slip a profanity!

My wife tackled me,
we fell to the ground
she was struck temporarily silent
from her happiness found.

"Is it you? Is it you?
Returned to me from the dead?"

"My Butterfly, I never left you,
no more tears should you shed!"

All at once my village went into motion,
all came from their homes
to see the cause of the commotion.

All came to greet me—
my name they all chanted—
I will never again
take my peoples' love for granted

All were curious and all had to ask
how I survived the last battle
to tell the tale if up to the task.

Any questions had to wait till tomorrow
for my wife had some of my time to borrow.

"Baby Wolf, before you last left,
I had more to tell you
but I wished not to distract you,
more than I usually do.
Before I say more,
promise one thing."

"Anything, my love,"

"Baby Wolf, learn how to sing.
Baby Wolf," my wife whispered,
"You are to be a father in Spring."

I hold her close.
The journey we were on
I now understood.
Young one, I finally know who you were
and this is good.

My thoughts drift
as I look across the water
and think to myself,
"Thank you for saving me,
my daughter!"

O' I learned how to dance,
I learned how to sing,
I learned all I could
before the next Spring.

You arrived in the Spring.
I was never this nervous in battle,
but I steadied myself,
yes, I made you your rattle!
The first time I held you
o' my heart did race!
As I looked upon you I said,
"I remember your face!"

Time went by…
this journey was at its end
I sit on the beach
holding my best friend.
My daughter, I thought you should know
I will always love and protect you
as you do grow.

I now sit with you on the shore,
happier now than known before.
I sing the song you once recited,
hearing you sing once again
very much invited.
Your mother and I
named you our Jewel.
Just to get you to smile
your proud father would act like a fool.
With you in my arms,
father and daughter
sit by the ocean.
Little one, do you know
what you have set into motion?
I want your new eyes
to only see peace,
for just by being,
you have given my life new lease—
I am on the right path
because of your insight,
and I promise to make
all my wrongs right,
so here we are
here by the sea.
I hold you now,
my daughter,
because you first
held me.

ONE LAST LESSON

Today is a most special day,
a grand potlatch and festivities
well under way.

A majority of clans
now stand as one.
Hostilities towards each other
we now shun.

My best friend Raven Smoke
has arrived,
countless battles together
we have fought and survived

They beach their canoes,
my family run up to greet
the most intimidating of warriors
you will happen to meet.

Raven Smoke is still adjusting to peace,
yet he forgets of battle
when dealing with his niece.

"Uncle! Uncle!"
my Jewel does shout.

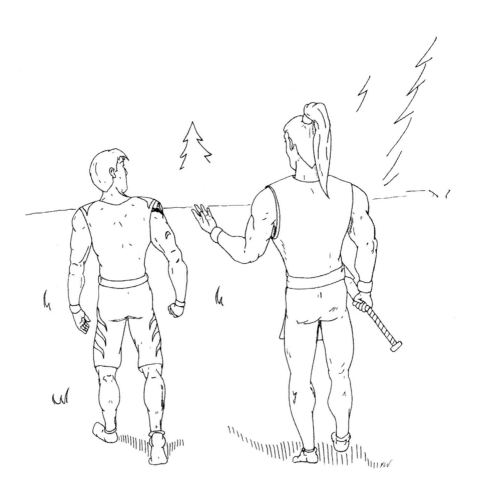

"My little Mischief!"
Raven Smoke laughs out.

In this time of peace
Jewel has played her part,
mostly by melting
the most icy of heart.

She jumps up and gives her uncle
a hug and kiss.
This reminds the great warrior
why battle you should never miss.

We walk the path
discussing present and past.
Near the end
Raven Smoke says at last,

"Baby Wolf,
I know how important it is
to unite the clans,
but remember, my friend,
peace can fail
even with the best laid plans."

"I know, my friend,
but have faith
and stay steady."

He replies,
"Old friend,
I hope you have kept
your blade arm ready."

I have known him for years—
sometimes difficult to read—
but looking upon him,
he is serious indeed.

"Baby Wolf, a clan to the North
was to have met us
but failed to show,
of their whereabouts
we do not know.
We have sent messengers
but none have come back—
I fear that they may have come
under attack."

I took a moment
let it sink in—
suddenly my faith
had begun to wear thin.

"Raven Smoke, then today must go well.
Only the chiefs and the elders
must we tell.
Peace through this land
is what we must first create
then tomorrow, old friend,
we will determine the lost clans
fate."

Raven Smoke thankfully agreed,
I prayed to the Spirits
that one day
is all we would need.

We entered the Great House
where the potlatch was in full swing.
Our women prepared every food
and did not miss a thing!

My sisters, Happy Brook and Little Princess,
are in the middle of others
preparing the feast—
the number of people before them
worries them not in the least.
Both are different
yet match one another.
Each a compliment
to our much missed mother.

Our father, Father Raven, is never too loud,
he seems even quieter when in a crowd.
He hides emotions well, in a shroud.
I hope to one day
make him proud.

My path as a warrior
caused him much dismay,
always quick to remind me
"That should not be your way!"

I have changed much
Since the birth of my child,
yet his opinion of me
still comes off as mild.

I teach the path of peace
from morning to sunset,
but his only words to me are
"Redemption is not yours yet."

60

We inform the elders
of the missing clan—
as expected, though,
all say
"Go forward with this day's plan."

I smile and greet elders and family
but as I cross the floor,
something makes me
look back to the door.
Yes, my armor hung there
shield and blade at the ready
something...something
made my heart unsteady.

Many a clan were in this Great House,
but most important to me
were my child and spouse.

My uneasiness made me
seek their well being.
They were with Raven Smoke
this was well worth seeing.

The elders and chiefs gathered,
and before the feast
it would be announced
that a peace between all clans
shall be pronounced!

The elders gathered together
to finally address us,
when suddenly my nephew, Clever Raven,
burst through the door
and kicked up a fuss.
He was out of breath and very confounded
"What is it, my nephew?!"

"Sir! We are surrounded!"
I ran to the door to see what I could.
More than two hundred warriors entrapped us—
no, this was not good.

Before any could ask the obvious
"What do they want?"
Their leader stepped forward and gave us his taunt.

"We received your invite
and thought it only polite
to personally tell you
your vision of peace is both
hypocritical and contrite!
Yes, you cry peace! It's so easy to say
especially since you and yours
have always had your way!

You've claimed lands and belongings
as you've seen fit
and if not given willingly
you've simply taken it!
Yes, your offer of peace does sound inviting,
but my trust in your people
I seem to be fighting!"

My uncle stepped forward,
chief of our clan,
"Enough! Young warrior, what is it you plan?!"

"Plan?!" Their leader cries, "Plan?!"
"Why, great chief, ease your fears,
we're here but for one man!"

The house fell silent,

who they wanted, none could distinguish—
whose life this day did they want to extinguish?

My wife and daughter crept to my side.
Looking upon them, their fear they could not hide.
Their leader then hollered with a mighty shout,
"Baby Wolf! Baby Wolf!
I recommend you step out!"

I am a warrior first and foremost—
never claimed to be the greatest,
but better than most.

I look to my wife, then to my daughter,
and the cold truth is
if they attack, we're defenseless,
it will be a slaughter.

I walk to the entrance,
make eye contact with my opponent,
"I'll be right out, give me one moment!"

"Yes! Yes! Say your good-byes,
but hurry up!
I have no patience or time for any more lies!"

I turn to my family, experience emotions
long not felt, the last moments of life
about to be dealt.

I hold my wife and child, those I hold most dear,
I attempt to sound brave,
"My loves, have not a fear."

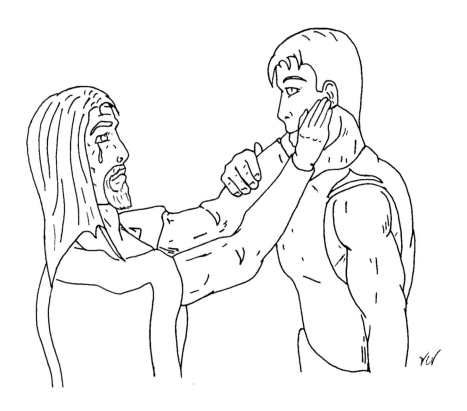

Raven Smoke walks up and extends his oversized hand,
"Come, my brother, let us make our last stand!"

"No, no, my friend
lower your axe.
This is not your end—
you will not pay this tax."

I shake his hand
I've never seen him this shaken,
"Brother, please know your friendship's
never been forsaken."

Though it pains him,
he manages a halfhearted smile;
I turn and prepare to walk
the long mile.

My father steps forward
puts his hands on my face,
"My son, my son, I have something to
tell you before you go."

"Rest easy, Father. I know, I know."
I hurry myself and walk away
part of me fearing what my father has to say.

"I'm proud of you!
I'm proud of you, my son!
I'm proud of who you are,
and all that you've done!"

After all this time,
after many a year,
this was all that I needed to hear.

I turn and give him
the happiest smile—
I wish I had more time
just to reconcile.

My father then said, with tears in his eyes,
"When you return, we shall take a long walk,
when you return, we'll have our long overdue talk!"

From outside my foe cries out,
"Baby Wolf! I grow tired of waiting!
Do you lack your courage?
Is that what you are debating?"

I walk to the door
where my sisters are in wait;
they prepare my armor
and wish to help prepare me for my fate.

I look to my sisters,
beauty like the dawn
lumps in their throats
they say, "Brother, put your armor on."
I give them both a hug and kiss
and look across the room
at new friends and new family.

"This is what I'll miss."

I shake my head, pick up my blade,
"My armor will not save me this day,
dear sisters, please put that away."

"Uncle, please! At least take your shield!"
cried Clever Raven, my nephew, predecessor,
and best on the training field.

I stand before him, have with him a last word,
"Dear nephew, I hope you remember all that I've taught
so that one day in this situation, you'll never be caught.
Nephew, stay strong, I must go face my fate.
Always remember,
never give in to hate.
Dear nephew it is now you that I beseech—
Clever Raven, pay attention
I have one last lesson to teach."

I step outside, my heart sank.
Warriors surrounded the Great House
and covered the sea bank.

I look across the great line—
they seem taken aback—
a lone warrior came to face them
and armor he did lack.
My foe shouted
"Is this a trick or a final insult?!
If you seek admiration, I fear you won't like the result!"

I take several steps forward and make my address,
"It's easy to speak bravely with numbers like yours
face you, young whelp, I'll do without remorse.
Before we fight though,
answer me this:

Are you the reason the clan from the North is amiss?"
An honest look of confusion crossed my opponent's face—
any hint of deceit
I could not trace.

"I know not of which you speak.
Step forward and face me—
you stall, for you are weak!"

It wasn't them? Then who, what, where, when, why?
I won't get my answers, for I am about to die.

"Young man, leave here now,
for you will find no glory.
Leave here now and there will be more to your story!"

The young warrior took a defiant step toward me,
his sheer size alone
told me of his family tree.

"Young man, I know who you are and what
this is about, will this ending be different?
That I very much doubt."

"Be quiet and fight! Prepare to face me!"

"Young man, your father, Eagle Claw, how is he?"

That is all it took.
A verbal slap upside his head—
"That's it, Baby Wolf, now you are dead!"
My young foe screamed,
his outer calmness
not as it seemed.

"You left him to die,
but you only did maim.
It's because of you
my father's forever lame!
Curse you! Curse you!
I curse your name,
for you are the cause of my family's shame!"

Eagle Claw's son was through with morality
charged straight and headlong
to test our mortality.

I took a deep breath,
all I've learned led to this:
Eagle Claw's son hurled a spear—
it passed and hissed—
I knelt down and I charged,
he was surprised that he missed.

He'd thrown the next spear with twice the strength
missed yet again,
it shot through a thick totem half length.
He drew his blade,
raised his shield,
we both ran full sprint across the field.
The outcome of this
to be determined by our blade,
yet in the back of my mind I hear
"Keep your promises made!"

As we lunge at each other
we both must take care,
for the slightest mistake
neither must dare.

He leaps in the air,
raises his blade for attack—
I duck beneath him—
let my blade go
and hear a sickening crack.

The young warrior takes a few steps past me
and falls down face first,
his clan lets out cries of anguish
for they fear the worst.

But before they have time
to even react,
the boy does stir
the young man's still intact!

I'm in front of the line, throw my blade in the ground,
"It is my turn to speak
let no one make a sound!
I knew of this day it haunts my dreams,
trust me my brothers, all is not as it seems.
Look towards my house
you'll see something I've made for you,
look in your hearts,
You'll see what I'm about to say true!"

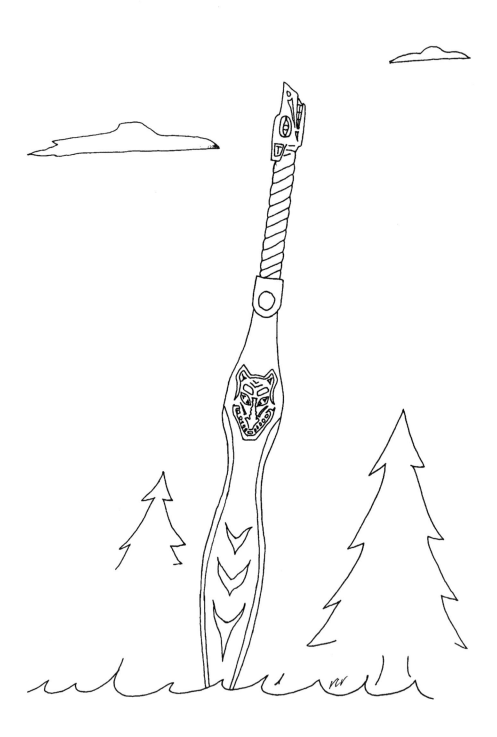

The line turned as one
and did happen to see
a beautiful totem that there ever would be.
Just a beautiful totem never meant to have a name,
just a beautiful totem,
my totem of shame.

"I've wronged you, my brothers,
I have no excuse.
You never deserved the wars or the abuse.
Take my life and spare all others.
Please forgive me,
forgive me, my brothers,
this is not our path, this is not our way.
Please do with me what you will,
but give peace a say!
I carved you that totem
to show my regret,
I know my brothers, I've not repaid
my debt yet."

Eagle Claw's son stood,
legs very weary,
removed my blade from the ground
my future indeed dreary.
He stood before me, raised my blade for the kill.

"After giving me my deserving end,
do me a favor, my young friend."

"What?" with animosity his reply came.

"Burn my totem of shame,
that's the spot I hope my ashes are laid
I pray you and yours consider my debt paid."

The young warrior's arm started to flex
yes, I knew what was to come next…

"Hold!"
A mighty voice shouted out
and with much authority,
gave the order
"Fall out!"

The men fell out of line
and moved gracefully apart,
who then approached me,
but this clan's soul and heart.

He now walked with a hitch
and needed full use of a cane,
Eagle Claw stood before me
the man I had almost slain,

His son stepped aside
remembering his place.
There we were now,
face to face.

He looked upon me
showing signs of great scorn,
but much more prominent
was the look of being torn.

Eagle Claw reaches over
takes from his son my blade
looks upon it,
"Yes…very well made."

He took my blade,
masterfully flipped it,
and presented it to me by its hilt.

"Killing you would only cause guilt.
My name is Eagle Claw,
chief of my clan.
You, I know, are Baby Wolf
but you are not the same man."

He moves past me and addresses
our people in the Great House,

"My brothers and sisters,
the Northwest is where we are from,
my apologies for this morning's actions
and I hope we are still welcome!"

Jubilant roars of cheers let out
and thunderous applause
for another great clan was brought to the fold
with peace being its main cause.

Eagle Claw then said to me,
"Baby Wolf, You have spared my son.
A great favor to me
is what you just have done.
That totem of yours, though,
will stay awhile longer.
It will stay
'til my faith in you
grows stronger!"
I smile and accept his outstretched hand.
Peace, glorious peace,
was to fill this land!

My family ran to my side
hugged and kissed me—
a better ending for a warrior
there could never be!

Now what was the lesson
I was hoping to teach?
What was the point
I was hoping to reach?

Young warriors who read this,
remember this tale, remember it well,
and in life, you will not fail.
In life it matters not what armor you wear,
it matters most what you can teach and share.

Life at times may never seem fair.
Remember, young warriors,
live life with great care.
At the end of this tale
and all its accounts,
remember, young warriors,
remember

What is inside your heart
is all that truly counts.

BABY WOLF

PREVIEW:

BABY WOLF—THE BAY OF DEATH

WRETCHED SOUND

The young woman runs
through the dark forest,
her daughter in tow
and youngest son to her chest.

She says in a whispered cry,
"Keep up! Keep up!
Follow Uncle's trap line!
Please, child, hurry
and everything will be fine!"

The trio move
as fast as they can
the mother fights through thoughts of

"We are the last of our clan!"

They arrive at the end of their uncle's lines—
only a few more hours
'til the sun once again shines.

The line ends at the shore bank
a canoe is there waiting,
all spirits she does thank.

She sets the canoe adrift,
loads her children and prepares to push from shore,
but suddenly realizes in her haste
she failed to grab an oar!

She leaps from the canoe
into the ice cold water
and moves with great haste.
The lives of her children hang in the balance
so time she cannot waste.

She grabs the oar, turns toward her children,
then from behind her came
a wretched sound.
She has heard this once before this night,
terror makes her turn around—

She raises her oar in brave attempt
to face her short future as it lies—

the last thing the poor mother sees

are terrible, wicked eyes...

To Be Continued

ABOUT THE AUTHOR

Victor Davis was born and raised in Petersburg, Alaska, and is a proud member of the Shangukeidi clan. He currently resides in Anchorage, Alaska, with his wife Yabba.

"The story of Baby Wolf is told from my life experiences, good and bad, a diary so to speak. Naturally, some of the story is embellished a bit, but remains true to its origins. What you may find interesting is this—some of the story's most extraordinary events represent things that have actually taken place in my life, while other ordinary events, simply represent my hopes and dreams. I hope you enjoy reading it as much as I enjoyed writing it!"

ORDER FORM

I would like to order my own or another copy of the book *Baby Wolf—A Warrior's Tale* by Victor Davis. Please send me:

_____# books x $16.95 per copy =   _____

+ Postage (first class) & handling @ $4.95/book: _____

TOTAL ENCLOSED $ _____

We accept cash, check, or money order made out to Northbooks, or VISA, Mastercard. Prices subject to change without notice.

(You may phone your VISA/MC order to Northbooks at 907-696-8973)

VISA/MC card # ☐☐☐☐ ☐☐☐☐ ☐☐☐☐ ☐☐☐☐

Exp. date: ___/_____   Amount charged: $ _____

Signature: _____

Phone number: _____

<u>Please send my book (s) to:</u>

Name: _____

Address: _____

City: _____ State: _____Zip: _____

Fill out this order form and send to:

Northbooks
17050 N. Eagle River Loop Rd, #3
Eagle River, AK 99577-7804
(907) 696-8973
www.northbooks.com

Printed in the United States
128189LV00002B/1/P